For Eunice and the badgers

Katherine Tegen Books is an imprint of HarperCollins Publishers.
Freddy & Frito and the Clubhouse Rules
Copyright © 2015 by Alison Friend

Library of Congress Cataloging-in-Publication Data
Friend, Alison.
    Freddy & Frito and the clubhouse rules / by Alison Friend. — First edition.
        pages cm
    Summary: Best friends Frito and Freddy want a place where they can play together that has plenty of space and not too many rules, so they build a clubhouse that is perfect—until their families and friends come to visit.
    ISBN 978-0-06-228580-5 (hardcover)
    [1. Clubhouses—Fiction. 2. Best friends—Fiction. 3. Friendship—Fiction. 4. Rules (Philosophy)—Fiction. 5. Family life—Fiction. 6. Animals—Fiction.] I. Title.
PZ7.F915225Fre 2015   2014005871
[E]—dc23   CIP
                                                                                                                        AC

The artist used pencil drawings with digital color to create the illustrations for this book.
Typography by Rachel Zegar
15   16   17   18   19   SCP   10   9   8   7   6   5   4   3   2   1
❖
First Edition

FREDDY & FRITO
and the Clubhouse Rules

By Alison Friend

KATHERINE TEGEN BOOKS
An Imprint of HarperCollins Publishers

Frito and Freddy
played together every day.

Some days they played at Freddy's,
where it was big and full of space.
"One, two, three! Jumping Jelly Beans!"
they screamed.

But there were RULES!

"Don't make a mess!" shouted Freddy's mom.

"And keep the noise down!"

Other days they played at Frito's, where it was noisy
and crowded with stuff everywhere.
    "Ahoy, you landlubbers!" hollered Captain Freddy.
    "Hand over yer cookies!" screamed One-Eyed Frito.
    "Rock Star Pirates to the rescue!"

But there were RULES!

"Don't use my pj's for a sail!"
Frito's dad yelled.

"And don't forget to
include your sisters!"

One very noisy day, Frito called Freddy.
"Can I come over and play?"

But Freddy's mom had just cleaned
and Great-Aunt Bernice was coming
over for lunch.

"I'm sorry, Frito," Freddy said.
"My mom said no."

"Oh, drat!" said Frito. "How
about we meet in the park instead?"

They met under a tree in the park exactly halfway between. It was 86 steps from Freddy's house and 124 steps from Frito's—because Frito's legs were a bit shorter, of course.

They searched for the perfect spot.

"I wish we had a place of our own,"
said Freddy, "a place that isn't always tidy!"
"Or too crowded!" said Frito.

"And somewhere not too small!" said Freddy.
"Or too noisy!" said Frito.

"Or too dark!"

"Why don't we build a clubhouse in this tree?" said Freddy.
"A place where we can play our games. Shout and scream.
Or even take a nap. A place with no rules!" squealed Frito.
"Definitely no rules!" Freddy agreed.

They began to collect things: Frito's mom gave them a big cardboard box and let Frito take his favorite cooking pot. Great-Aunt Bernice gave Freddy some yellow curtains, and Uncle Monty found them a tattered umbrella. Kind Mrs. Winkle from across the street donated cushions, some blankets, and half a bicycle!

They got to work. First they made walls from cardboard—leaving holes for windows.

Then came a roof in case it rained.

Next they banged two pieces of wood together to make a door. Soon the place was shaping up!

"We'll put my bed right here!" Freddy said.

"My pirate ship, too!" said Frito.

"That's too big!" yelled Freddy.

"A pirate ship is supposed to be big!" Frito yelled back.

"Your yellow curtains are giving me a headache!" Frito complained.

"And your cooking pot is disgusting and stinky!" said Freddy. Then he tossed the pot out the door into the mud.

"That's rude!" Frito cried. And he pulled down the yellow curtains and jumped up and down on them. Then he ran home, crying.

"There's not enough room in our clubhouse for all our stuff,"
Frito told his mom. "And Freddy thinks his things are more
important than mine. He threw my cooking pot into the mud!"

"Oh, Sweet Pea!" said his mom. "Houses are never big enough."
She gave him a big hug.

Freddy ran home, too.

"All the stuff we need won't fit inside our clubhouse, Mom!" he explained. "And Frito's things are big and smelly!" Then Freddy burst out crying, too.

His mom gave him a squeeze and told him that all best friends fight— but they always work things out.

The next day they both came back with the same idea.

"Let's make the place bigger!" said Frito.

"A lot bigger!" said Freddy. "Big enough for your pirate ship AND my bed!"

"And," they both agreed, "big enough for a huge party!"

They worked and they worked and they worked all day. Finally, it was finished.

Freddy delivered invitations for a clubhouse-warming party to take place that very afternoon.

Frito made lemonade and mud pies.
The weather was perfect!

At four o'clock, there was a line of guests winding out of the park gates and around the block. Everyone wanted to see inside the clubhouse. No one knew what to expect.

The party guests were having a great time. "No rules! No rules!" squealed Frito's cousins, throwing mud pies at each other. Frito tried hard not to watch his delicious mud pies going to waste, and Freddy tended to a crying hedgehog. Both boys could hardly believe their eyes when Tiggy Winkle blew her nose on the curtains.

"Wanna play Rock Star Pirates?" Freddy asked Frito. But Uncle Monty was singing opera to a ship full of squirrels while the twins from next door slid down the mast—taking the sail down with them!

"How about Jumping Jelly Beans?" asked Frito. But Cousin Barnaby was bouncing on the bed with the badger brothers and their very muddy paws.

"Oh no!" said both boys when they noticed that their shortsighted neighbor, Douglas, had mistaken Frito's cooking pot for the bathtub.

"We need an emergency meeting!" declared Frito.

So both boys scrambled up to the top floor.

"What can we do, Freddy? We can't play
our own games. It's way too noisy!"
"Everyone's being crazy! When will they
all go home?"
How could they get the guests to leave?

They had the perfect idea.

They found Frito's cooking pot and made their guests a special dinner.

"One bucket of pond water," said Frito.

"An old shoe, a dead fish," said Freddy, "and throw in some moldy cheese!"

Frito stirred the stinky mixture, and Freddy set the table with the yellow curtain.

"You must stay and eat with us, everybody!" shouted Freddy. "It's Clubhouse Special Stew!"

But before Frito dished out the first bowlful, the guests began to leave.

"Sorry, boys. We have to get your sisters to bed!" said Frito's mom.

"Sorry! Our dad said be back by six," said the badger brothers.

"Thank you for inviting me, but I think I left my oven on!" said Great-Aunt Bernice.

Now everyone was gone, and the clubhouse
had just the right amount of noisy and just the right
amount of quiet. They played Jumping Jelly Beans
and Rock Star Pirates, and even took a snooze.

"Maybe we should have just one rule,"
said Freddy.
    They both thought for a minute, and
then gave each other a wink.

That was the only rule they needed.